Too TALL to Twirl

BONNEY PRESS

Published by Bonney Press,
an imprint of Hinkler Books Pty Ltd
45–55 Fairchild Street
Heatherton Victoria 3202 Australia
www.hinkler.com

BONNEY PRESS

Illustration: Anna Shuttlewood
Text: Lisa Regan
Design: Bianca Zuccolo
Prepress: Graphic Print Group

ISBN: 978 1 4889 3222 9

Printed and bound in China

Too
TALL
to
Twirl

It was a fine day, and Giraffe was out walking with her friend, Owl. Giraffe was looking thoughtful.

'Owl,' she said. 'Do you have a hobby? I wish I did. Everyone else has something they do for fun.'

'Then why don't you join them?' said Owl. 'You can see what suits you.'

Giraffe lolloped off. She found Hippo practising her ballet moves, and enjoying herself very much. 'Hmm,' thought Giraffe, 'what about ballet?'

'Can I try?' asked Giraffe. 'Of course!' called Hippo.
Hippo twirled gracefully across the plains.

WHEEEEE!

Giraffe looked worried. Was she too tall to twirl?

'I don't know if ballet is for me,' she murmured. 'But I'll try.'

She took a step with one long left leg. So far, so good.

But then she tried to jump her right foot
in front of her left, and...

...WAAAH!

Giraffe decided to keep looking. Soon she saw Ostrich swooping and swirling on her skates.

'Can I have a go?' asked Giraffe.
'Just grab some skates!' called Ostrich.

Giraffe felt anxious as she fastened the skates to her feet. 'This does look very tricky,' she muttered. 'But if Ostrich can do it with her long legs, then surely I can do it too.'

She bent her legs and tried to stand up straight.
Slooooowly does it...

...OOOPS!

Giraffe crept away. 'Finding a hobby is not easy at all,' she said sadly. At that moment, Giraffe spotted her friend Antelope balancing upon some fallen logs.

'Hey, Giraffe!' called Antelope. 'Give gymnastics a try!'
Antelope tumbled and flipped gracefully through the grass.

Giraffe wiggled her long neck and shook each of her long legs. She took a deep breath and tucked in her head for a forward roll.

She bent lower... and lower... and lower...

...OOF!

'Nope, gymnastics isn't for me either!' Giraffe said with a sigh.

'Don't despair,' roared Lion. 'Do a little dance!'
Lion strutted and shimmied. He was really very good.

Giraffe was nervous. Everything she had tried had gone so wrong! But she didn't want to give up. Giraffe took a deep breath, pointed her toes, stretched out her arms and leapt into the air.

'Look out, Lion!'

...OUCH!

Giraffe made a quick escape. Perhaps she was trying the wrong hobbies?

'Hey, Giraffe!' called Zebra. 'Karate is cool!'
Zebra spun in a circle and kicked out her hooves.

Giraffe agreed. It did look cool... and she had hooves, too. This could be her thing!

She stuck out one leg and swung around...

...EEK!

Giraffe slumped to the ground and hung her head. 'Hey, you!' hooted Owl. 'Why do you look so blue?'

Giraffe let out a big sigh. 'I'm no good at any of this! I'm too tall to twirl, and skate, and dance...'

Owl tutted. 'Everyone is good at something. Look at me – I can't fly fast, but I am extremely good at I-spy! We will find something you can do.'

Giraffe scrambled to her feet. Owl was very good at looking
at things in a positive way.
As Giraffe and Owl thought together, Giraffe noticed
something hurtling towards them. A bird? A bat? A... ball?

Quick as a flash, Giraffe head-butted it away, stopping Owl from being knocked off her branch, just in time.

'Wow!' called Hyena, who came racing after the ball.
'Nice save! You should be a goalkeeper!'

Giraffe was worried. She knew she was too tall to twirl...
was she too tall for this team?

The other players cheered her on. 'Join us! Come and play!'

So Giraffe trotted nervously onto the field. The game began and she leaped and soared and even twirled! No one could score against her. She was a superstar!

By the end of the game, Giraffe was tired but happy.
Everyone clapped and lifted her high in celebration.
'You're the perfect height to go in goal!'

Giraffe had finally found a hobby.